BY THE LIGHT
OF THE MOON

All inquiries should be addressed to:
Barron's Educational Series, Inc.
250 Wireless Boulevard
Hauppauge, NY 11788

International Standard Book Number 0-8120-1027-2

Library of Congress Catalog Card Number 94-73247

PRINTED IN HONG KONG
5678   9927   987654321

GET READY...GET SET...READ!

BY THE LIGHT
OF THE MOON

by
Foster & Erickson

Illustrations by
Kerri Gifford

BARRON'S

What do you see
by the light of the moon,

when the moon is full
like a round balloon?

I see a cocoon
by the light of the moon,

and think of what
it will look like soon.

I see a raccoon
as she finds a spoon,

near the dunes
by the light of the moon.

What do you hear
by the light of the moon,

when the day is over
and you first see the moon?

I hear a moose call.
It is like a bassoon.

I hear a loon
as she croons a tune.

What do you feel
by the light of the moon?

I feel warm under
the full June moon.

What do you say
by the light of the moon?

I say thank you for
the cocoon and the raccoon,
the moose and the loon,

when its quiet and still
by the light of the moon.

The End

The OON Word Family

balloon
bassoon
cocoon
croons
loon
moon
raccoon
soon
spoon

The UNE Word Family

dunes
June
tune

Sight Words

call
full
over
warm
first
light
quiet
round
think
under

Dear Parents and Educators:

Welcome to *Get Ready...Get Set...Read!*

We've created these books to introduce children to the magic of reading.

Each story in the series is built around one or two word families. For example, *A Mop for Pop* uses the OP word family. Letters and letter blends are added to OP to form words such as TOP, LOP, and STOP. As you can see, once children are able to read OP, it is a simple task for them to read the entire word family. In addition to word families, we have used a limited number of "sight words." These are words found to occur with high frequency in the books your child will soon be reading. Being able to identify sight words greatly increases reading skill.

You might find the steps outlined on the facing page useful in guiding your work with your beginning reader.

We had great fun creating these books, and great pleasure sharing them with our children. We hope *Get Ready...Get Set...Read!* helps make this first step in reading fun for you and your new reader.

Kelli C. Foster, Ph.D.
Educational Psychologist

Gina Clegg Erickson, MA
Reading Specialist

Guidelines for Using *Get Ready...Get Set...Read!*

Step 1.   Read the story to your child.

Step 2.   Have your child read the Word Family list
            aloud several times.

Step 3.   Invent new words for the list. Print each new
            combination for your child to read.
            Remember, nonsense words can be used
            (*dat, kat, gat*).

Step 4.   Read the story *with* your child. He or she reads
            all of the Word Family words; you read the rest.

Step 5.   Have your child read the Sight Word list
            aloud several times.

Step 6.   Read the story *with* your child again. This time
            he or she reads the words from both lists;
            you read the rest.

Step 7.   Your child reads the entire book to you!

There are five sets of books in the

Series. Each set consists of five **FIRST BOOKS**
and two **BRING-IT-ALL-TOGETHER BOOKS**.

SET 1

is the first set your children should read.
The word families are selected from the short vowel sounds:
at, **ed**, **ish** and **im**, **op**, **ug**.

SET 2

provides more practice
with short vowel sounds:
an and **and**, **et**, **ip**, **og**, **ub**.

SET 3

focuses on
long vowel sounds:
ake, **eep**, **ide** and **ine**, **oke** and **ose**, **ue** and **ute**.

SET 4

introduces the idea that the word family sounds
can be spelled two different ways:
ale/ail, **een/ean**, **ight/ite**, **ote/oat**, **oon/une**.

SET 5

acquaints children with word families that
do not follow the rules for long and short vowel sounds:
all, **ound**, **y**, **ow**, **ew**.